Blue Sea

by Robert Kalan

illustrated by
Donald Crews

 Greenwillow Books
A Division of William Morrow & Company, Inc., New York

COPY 4

10 9 8 7 6 5 4 3 2

Library of Congress
Cataloging in Publication Data
Kalan, Robert. Blue sea.
Summary: Several fishes of varying size introduce
space relationships and size differences.
[1. Size and shape—Fiction. 2. Space
perception—Fiction. 3. Fishes—Fiction]
I. Crews, Donald. II. Title. PZ7.K123475Bl
[E] 78-18396 ISBN 0-688-80184-6
ISBN 0-688-84184-8 lib. bdg.

For Aunt Helen and Uncle Steve
—R. K.
For Hidy and Slank
—D. C.

blue sea

little fish

big fish

swim, little fish

bigger fish

swim, big fish

swim, little fish

biggest fish

swim, bigger fish

swim, big fish

swim, little fish

small hole

there goes bigger fish

there goes big fish

there goes little fish

good-bye, biggest fish

Ouch!

good-bye, bigger fish

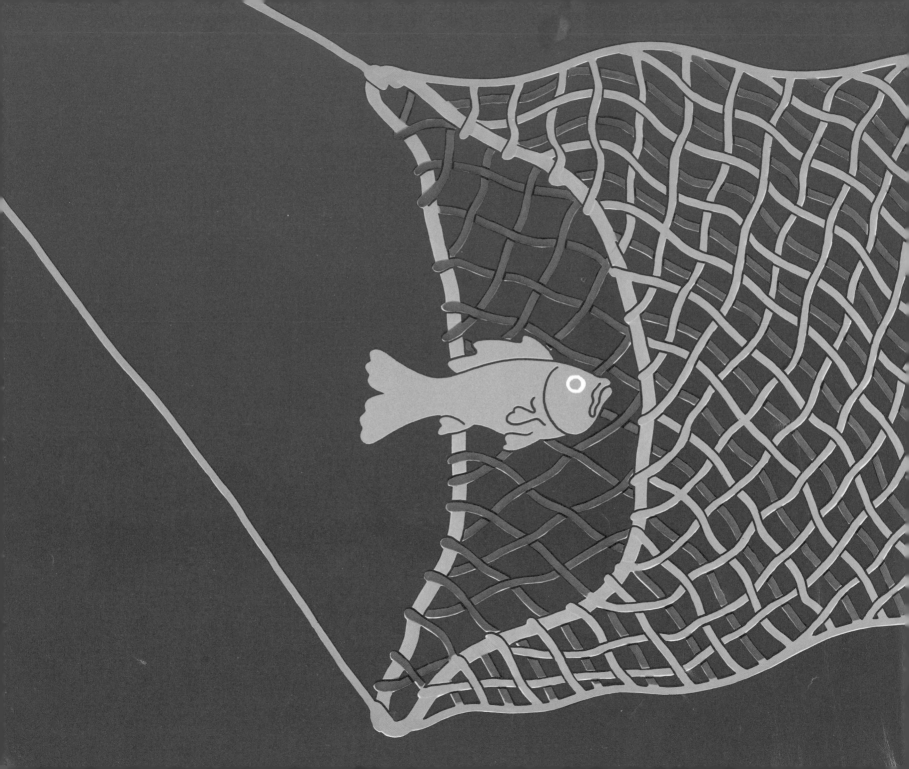

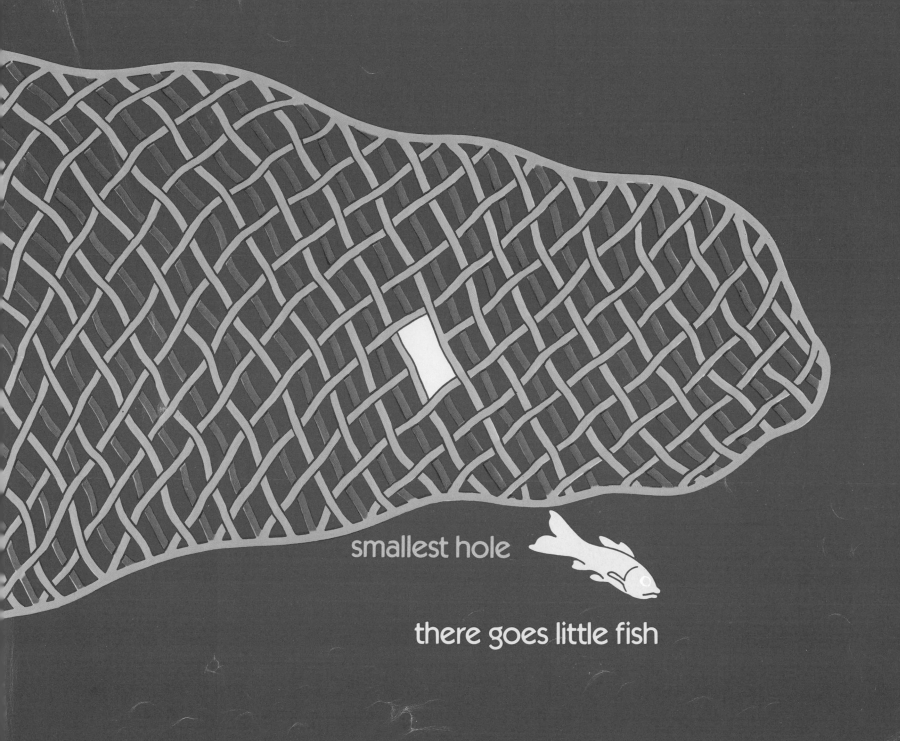

smallest hole

there goes little fish

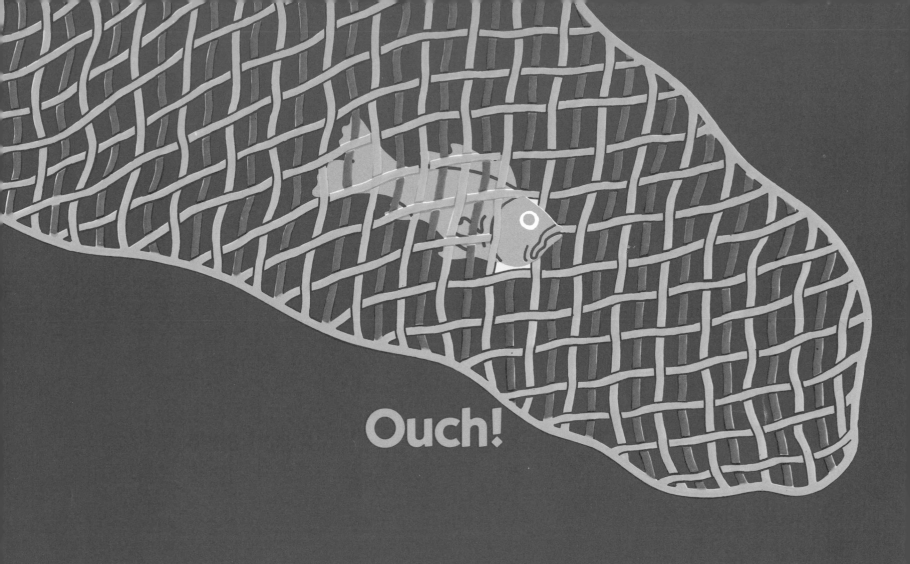

Ouch!

good-bye, big fish

little fish

blue sea

Robert Kalan

was born in Los Angeles. He was graduated from Claremont Men's College in 1972. He has taught reading to both gifted and remedial students as well as kindergarten and fourth grade, and completed a master's degree in education at Claremont Graduate School. He is currently living in Seattle, where he teaches a course in writing for children at the University of Washington. His first book was Rain, illustrated by Donald Crews.

Donald Crews

was graduated from Cooper Union for the Advancement of Science and Art in New York City. He has written and illustrated many books for young children, including We Read: A to Z and the more recent Freight Train, published by Greenwillow. He and his wife Ann are free-lance artists and designers, and live in New York with their two daughters.

COPY 4

JP/STORY
Kalan, Robert
Blue sea

DATE DUE	
APR 26 1994	
AUG 1 0 1994	
FEB 2 1997	
SEP 0 2 1997	
SEP 9 1998	
OCT 1 1998	
JUN 2 8 2000	
AUG 9 2000	
OCT 3 2000	
JUL 0 9 2001	
FEB 2 4 2003	
APR 1 2 2004	
JAN 1 9 2005	

GAYLORD   PRINTED IN U.S.A.